TOBY BELFER
and the
High Holy Days

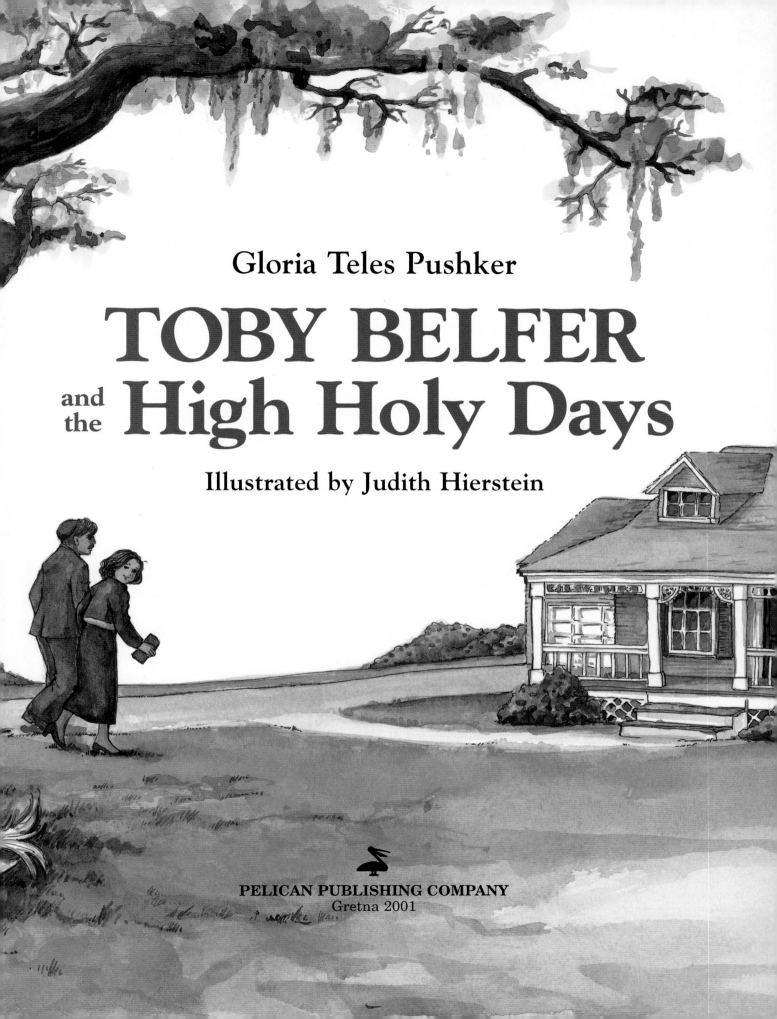

Gloria Teles Pushker

TOBY BELFER
and the High Holy Days
the

Illustrated by Judith Hierstein

PELICAN PUBLISHING COMPANY
Gretna 2001

To my aunt Adelaide—happy ninetieth birthday—and to Gerson
Special thanks to Rabbi Robert Loewy
Special thanks also to Louis Saltz for suggesting this book title

The word "Pelican" and the depiction of a pelican are trademarks
of Pelican Publishing Company, Inc., and are registered
in the U.S. Patent and Trademark Office.

Library of Congress Cataloging-in-Publication Data

Pushker, Gloria Teles.
    Toby Belfer and the High Holy Days / Gloria Teles Pushker ; illustrated by
Judith Hierstein.
        p. cm.
    Summary: Toby Belfer tells her non-Jewish friend Donna all about celebrating
Rosh Hashanah and Yom Kippur. Includes a recipe for honey cake.
    ISBN 1-56554-765-9 (alk. paper)
    [1. Rosh ha-Shanah—Fiction. 2. Yom Kippur—Fiction. 3. Fasts and
feasts—Judaism—Fiction. 4. Jews—United States—Fiction.] I. Hierstein,
Judy, ill. II. Title.
PZ7.P97943 Tl 2000
[E]—dc21
                                                                    99-089424

Printed in Hong Kong

Published by Pelican Publishing Company, Inc.
1000 Burmaster Street, Gretna, Louisiana 70053

TOBY BELFER AND THE HIGH HOLY DAYS

Toby Belfer was lying down on her porch swing with one arm under her head, the other arm covering her eyes, and her legs over the armrest. Her dog, Windy, was on the porch, too.

As the swing gently swayed, it seemed to her that the squeaky chains whispered, "Help one another. Help one another. Say you're sorry. Say you're sorry."

Toby's best friend, Donna Barker, came over and quietly watched Toby on the swing. She patted Windy's head.

Toby could feel Donna staring. She quickly sat up, making room for Donna on the swing. Toby said, "Donna, if I've done anything to hurt your feelings, I'd like to say I'm sorry."

Donna cried, "What in the world are you talking about, Toby Belfer? You are the best friend anyone could have."

"Thank you," replied Toby, "but I was just thinking about what the rabbi said in his sermon today for Rosh Hashanah. 'In the new year,' he said, 'we must help one another and be good citizens.' He told us the importance of giving charity and to be sure to apologize for anything that might have hurt someone."

"Donna, remember when I bumped into you playing soccer? I gave you a black eye. We lost the game, and I didn't even say I was sorry."

"I remember," answered Donna, smiling. "I forgive you, but that was an accident. In fact, your black eye was worse than mine. Will you forgive me?" They laughed.

Then Toby said thoughtfully, "Remember when I called your little brother *la biblioteca*? He ran home crying and I thought it was a big joke. It really wasn't funny. In fact, it was rude of me to tease him. Maybe he would like for me to read him some books from the school's library. Sometimes you should do more than just 'say' you're sorry."

"That's a great idea," said Donna. "I'm sure he'd like that."

The girls sat quietly. Toby said, almost in a whisper, "You know, Donna, I was very angry when my grandmother died last month. My parents explained that it was OK for me to feel that way for a little while. They said death is part of the life cycle and that Gram will live in my heart forever. I pray that God will forgive me for being so angry. I know that my prayers will make me feel better."

Donna said, "Tell me more about your holidays, Toby."

"Well," explained Toby, "today is Rosh Hashanah, the Jewish New Year—the birthday of the world. Our family got all dressed up last night and again this morning. We drove to the synagogue in the city.

"There is a prayer sung on Rosh Hashanah Eve called *Avinu Malkanu*—Our Father, Our King. That is my favorite!" Toby exclaimed. "The melody is so beautiful; I can't get it out of my head. After all the songs were sung and most of the prayers were heard, we heard the great sound of a ram's horn called a shofar. It is said that this celebrates God's closeness to us."

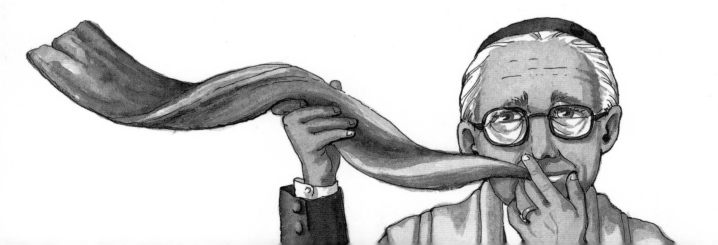

"The congregation then went into the reception hall, where everyone ate honey cake and tasted honey and apples for a sweet New Year." Toby wanted to lick her lips just remembering it. "We told each other, *'L'shanah Tovah.'* That's Hebrew for 'Happy New Year.'"

"Eight days from now, on Yom Kippur," Toby continued, "adults, as well as the kids who have been Bar or Bat Mitzvah, will fast by not eating or drinking anything from sundown to sundown. This is their way of saying they are sorry for promises broken and for breaking God's rules like honoring parents and teachers and being truthful. They are showing their repentance by fasting."

"Oh," said Donna, "I think I understand."

Toby smiled as she went on. "On the evening before Yom Kippur Day, the Holy Ark in the synagogue is opened. The Torah scrolls, covered in white velvet especially for the High Holy Days, are held by members of the congregation."

"The lights are dimmed and the beautiful ancient prayer *Kol Nidre* is heard three times," Toby said. "It is first chanted by the cantor, then repeated by the choir, then, in our synagogue, played on a violin. It is truly awesome. The words *Kol Nidre* mean 'all vows.' It says, 'From this day of atonement to the next, we do repent.' It asks God to hear our vows and forgive our sins."

"All day Yom Kippur, the congregation sits and prays, reflecting on the past year. There are special children's services and memorial services, too." Toby grew quiet now, thinking about these solemn services that would be coming soon.

"When the sun goes down, and the prayers have ended, the great sound of the shofar is heard once again." Toby imitated the sound for Donna.

"Friends and family join together to break the fast, but before we eat, more prayers are said," Toby continued. "We say, 'Baruch atah Adonai, Elohenu melech ha'olam, hamotsi lechem min ha oretz. Blessed art Thou, O Lord our God, Ruler of the universe, Who brings forth bread from the earth.' Everyone tastes the delicious bread called challah, baked especially to welcome holidays."

Toby could see that she was making Donna hungry.

"My dad says, 'Baruch atah Adonai, Elohenu melech ha'olam, bore pa-re hagafen. Blessed art Thou, O Lord our God, Ruler of the universe, Who created the fruit of the vine.' He takes a sip of wine." Toby made the motion. "That's when dinner is served."

As Toby and Donna sat on the porch and talked about Rosh Hashanah and Yom Kippur, they didn't notice that Windy was not beside them. When they realized this, Toby called to her, but Windy didn't come.

Toby thought she heard a whimpering sound coming from under the porch steps. The girls went to look and were greeted by the beautiful sight of Windy and her three fluffy new white puppies! They looked just like Windy.

Later that night when the Belfers' house was quiet, Toby went to her room and looked out of the window.

She could see millions of bright, shining stars in the Southern sky. She could smell the honeysuckle, and in the quiet, she could hear the puppies.

It had been a long day for Toby, but in retelling the story of Rosh Hashanah and Yom Kippur to Donna she learned a lot herself and thought how wonderful it is to have new life for a New Year.

L'shanah Tovah, y'all!

GRAM'S RECIPE FOR HONEY CAKE

1½ cups honey
1 cup oil
2 tsp. instant-coffee granules
½ cup boiling water
1¼ cups dark brown sugar
4 eggs
4 cups self-rising flour
1 heaping tsp. cinnamon
1 heaping tsp. mixed spices
1 level tsp. ginger
1 level tsp. baking soda

Beat together the honey and oil. Dissolve the coffee in the boiling water. Add the coffee water and sugar to the honey and oil and beat. Beat in the eggs. Sift together the dry ingredients and beat them into the wet ingredients. Line a shallow 12" x 10" x 3" tin pan with wax paper. Pour in the batter and bake at 325 degrees for 1 to 1¼ hours. When done, sprinkle with powdered sugar if desired.

GLOSSARY

BAR MITZVAH—A boy who has been admitted as an adult member of the Jewish community, usually at age thirteen during a special ceremony.

BAT MITZVAH—A girl who has been admitted as an adult member of the Jewish community, in some cases at age twelve, during a special ceremony.

BREAK THE FAST—Eat and drink for the first time in twenty-four hours at the end of Yom Kippur.

CANTOR—A person who chants and leads musical worship.

CHALLAH—Pronounced hallah; special bread prepared to welcome holidays.

KOL NIDRE—Hebrew for "all vows"; ancient prayer that ushers in Yom Kippur.

LA BIBLIOTECA—Spanish for "the library."

RABBI—A spiritual leader of Judaism.

ROSH HASHANAH—Jewish New Year, birthday of the world.

SHOFAR—Ram's horn.

TORAH—Handwritten scroll containing the first five books of the Bible.

YOM KIPPUR—The Day of Atonement.